STECK-VAUGHN
NEW WAY
HEADS and TAILS

The King

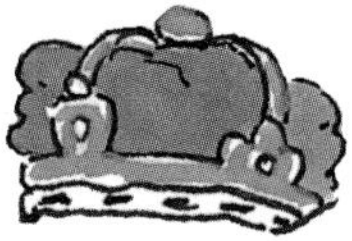

STECK-VAUGHN®
COMPANY

A Division of Harcourt Brace & Company

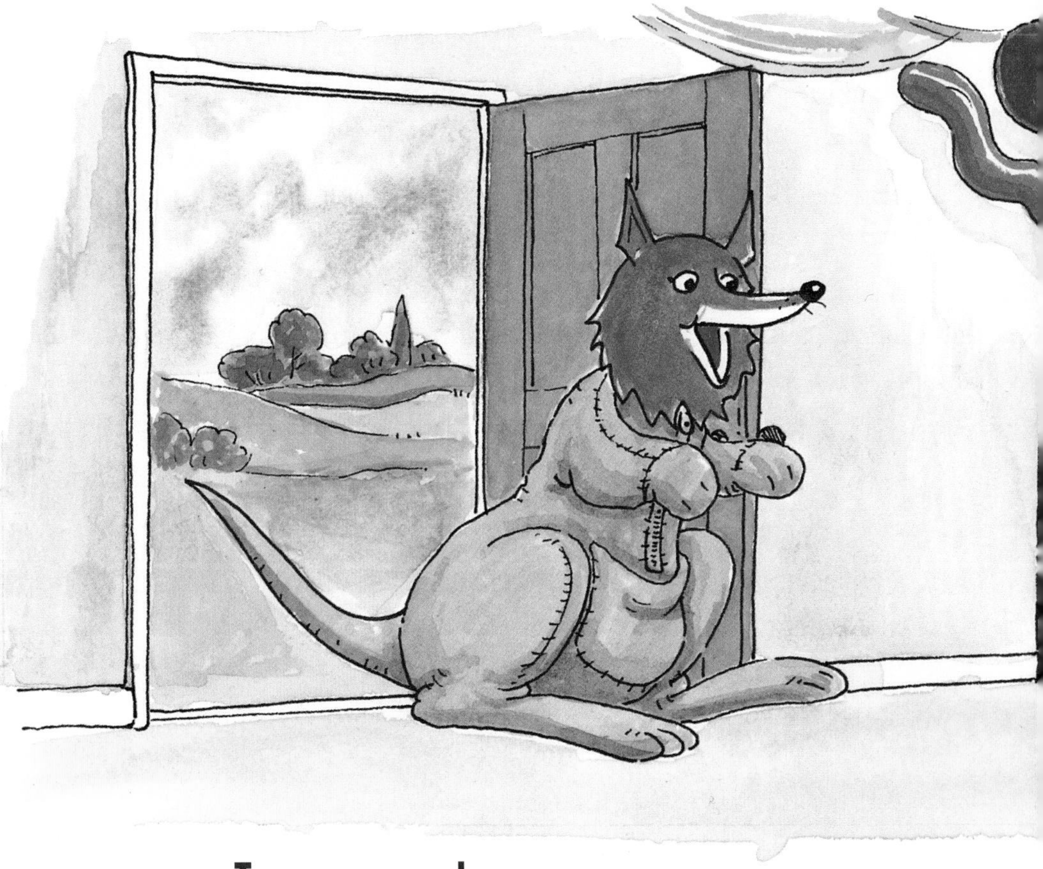

I am a kangaroo.

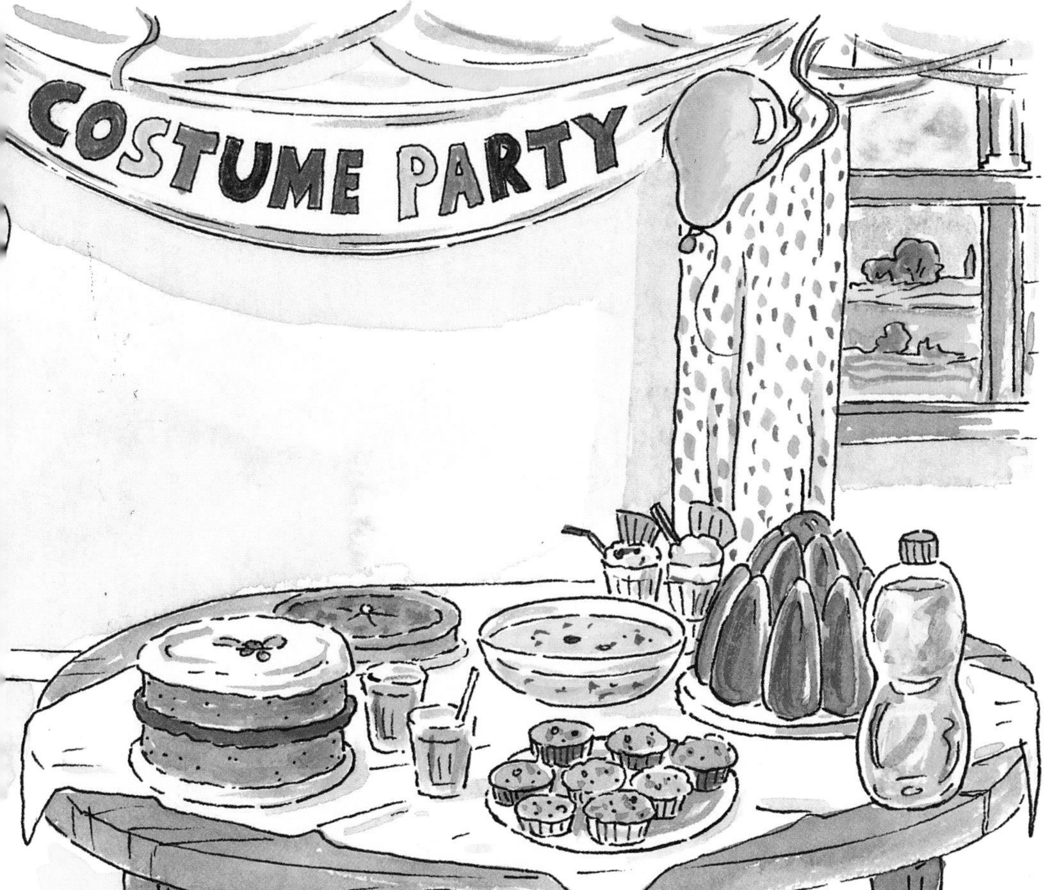
COSTUME PARTY

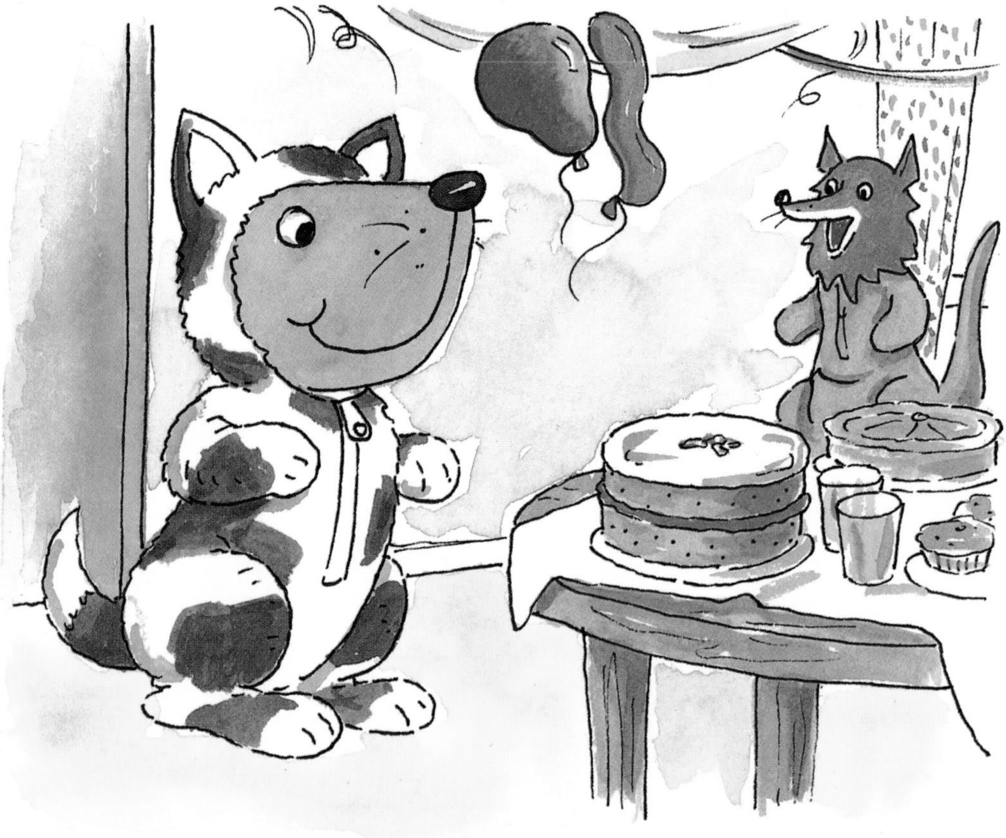

I am a kitten.

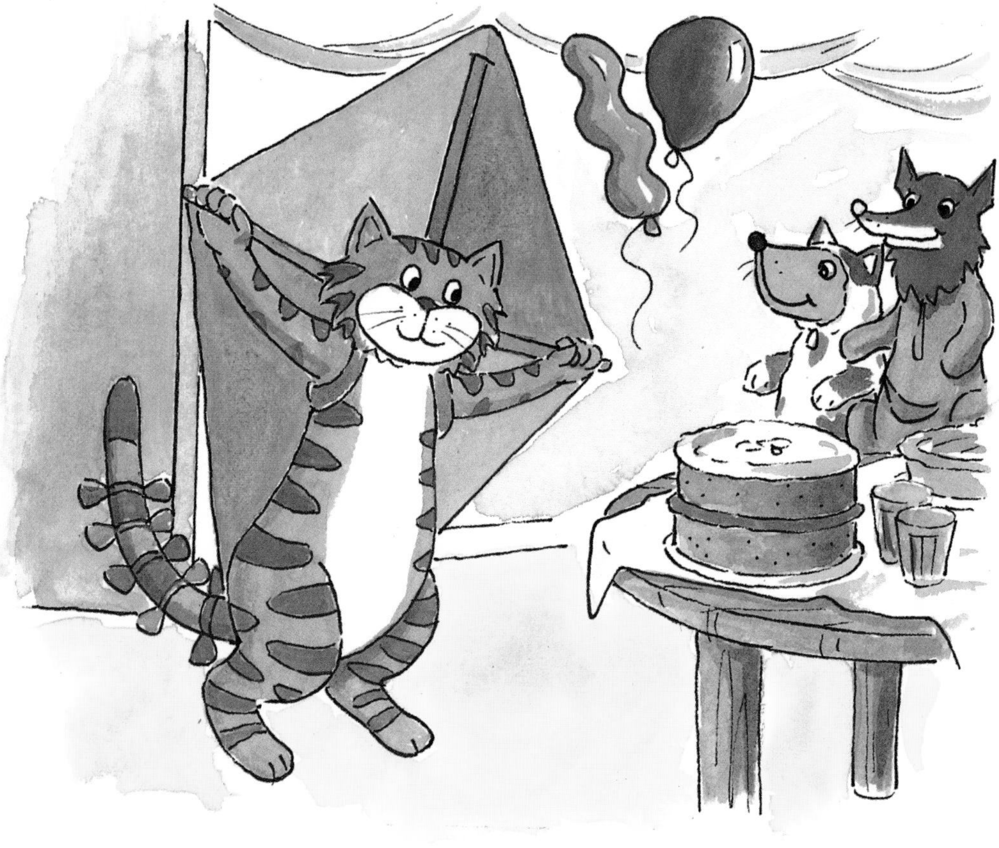

I am a kite.

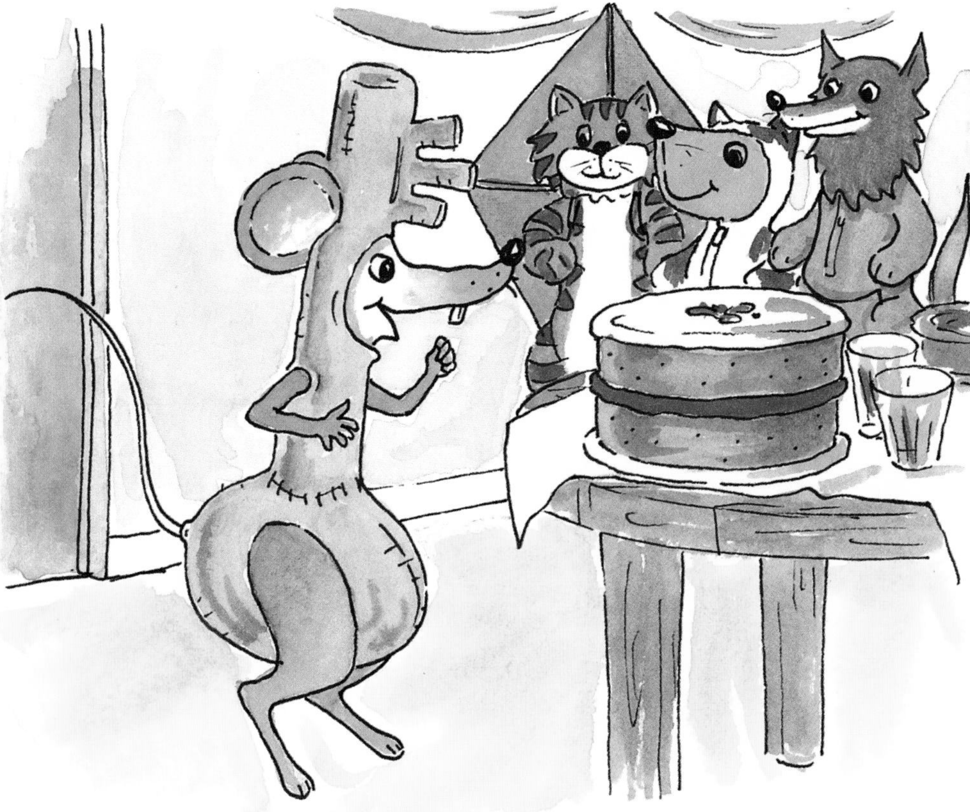

I am a key.

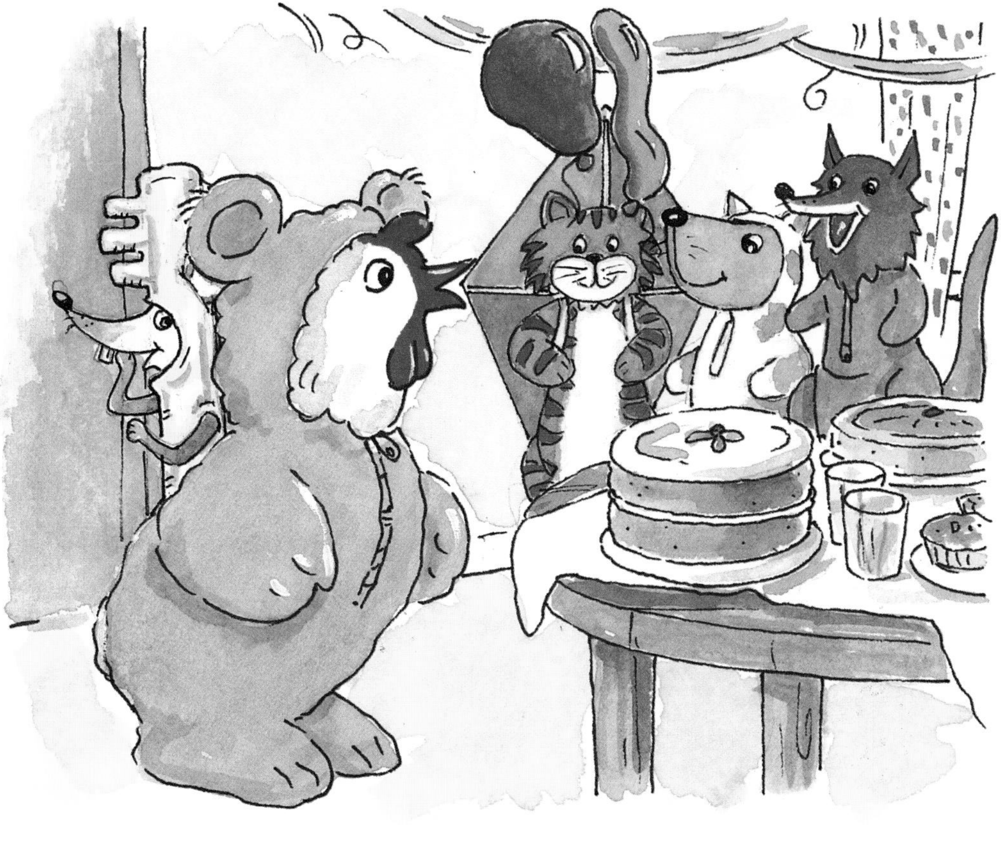

I am a koala.

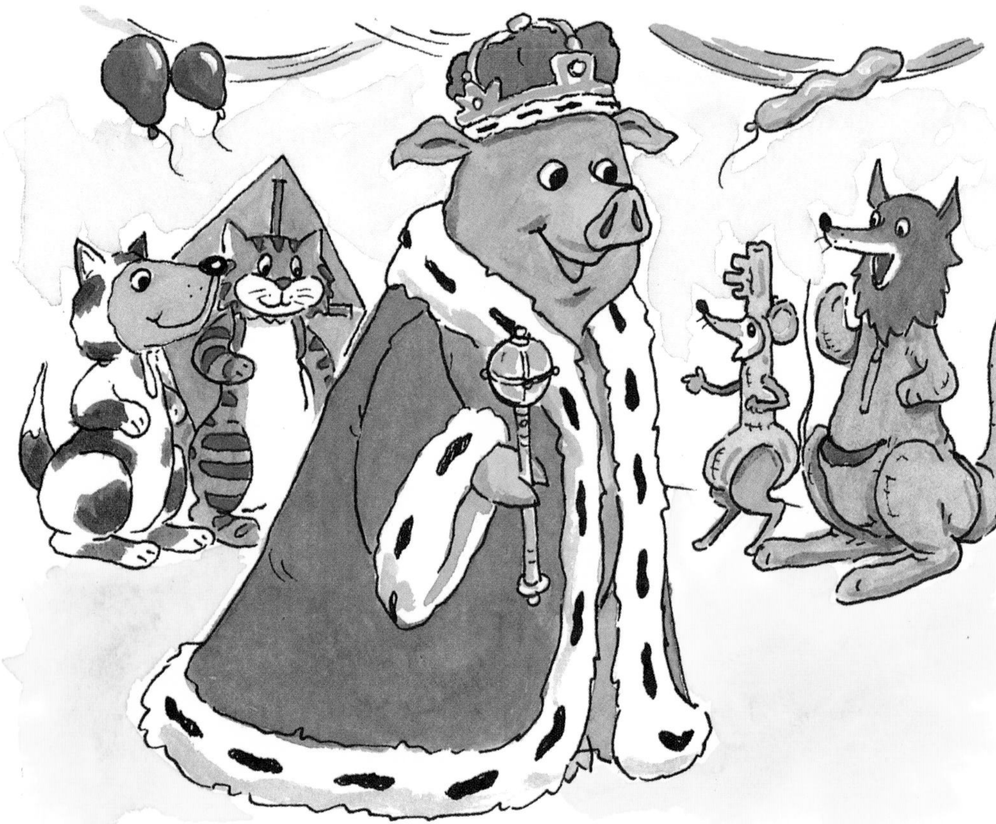

I am a king!